PICTURE KEY

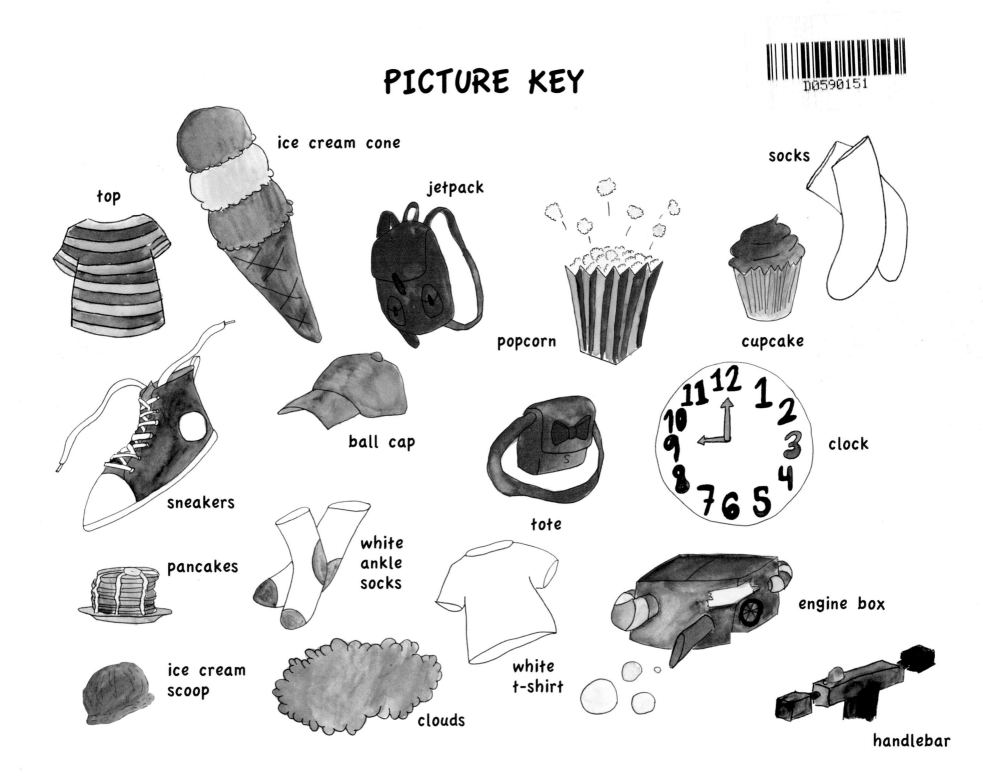

top

ice cream cone

jetpack

popcorn

socks

cupcake

sneakers

ball cap

tote

clock

pancakes

white ankle socks

white t-shirt

engine box

ice cream scoop

clouds

handlebar

Dedication Cloud

For Michael, Jake and Nick WITH ALL MY LOVE.
Without your encouragement, honesty and love,
this book would still be in my filing cabinet.

Missy, I am deeply grateful to your
unique contribution to this book,
and (especially) my life. *Thank you.*

Jocelyn, thank you for your masterful
editing skills to my manuscript,
(and that was when it was twice as long).

Trish, thank you for your complete honesty about this book.
You said exactly what I needed to hear.

And, to my darling sweet illustrator, Lauren... your creativity, ideas
(like these purple clouds) and love for JET & Scoot, brought them
PERFECTLY to life. With all my heart, merci beaucuop.
If feels like, we had our own Adventure-SUMMER,
learning how to create a children's illustration book
together. I hope we do it again next summer...XO

P.S. Cloud

And most importantly,
to all the readers, I hope
this book inspires
your very own
Adventure-Saturday

Design & Layout
Christian Prollamante
cprollamante.com

JET & Scoot

a story about us

It's
Adventure-Saturday!
JET & Scoot

are just about to start.
Are you ready?

Let's GO!

As soon as

JET & Scoot

wake up, they

greet each other

from their

bedroom windows

to give their

top-secret

hand signal.

Sitting on their favorite hillside, **JET** & Scoot and Tucker are huunnngry. They share a yummy 🧁 and frosty cold 🍾.

"This is just like downtown!" they both say.

"**JET**, Adventure-Saturday is MY favorite day of the week!" Scoot says cheerfully. "Adventure-Saturday is MY favorite day of the week too!" **JET** shouts!

With the mud rubbed off his face, **JET** scrambles out of the pond. Saying goodbye to their new friend **Ribbit**, **JET** & **Scoot** make their way back to their jetryde & pooSH bike. Tucker charges ahead with his usual get-up-and-go gusto.

JET shouts, "ALL righty gang, let's hit the open road for our Adventure-Saturday Finale!"

Scoot chirps, "Okey Dokey Artichoke-y!"

Tucker immediately goes 🍌 , surprising **JET**. Losing his balance, **JET** falls face-first into the 🌱 and launches the 🐸 up into the air. With mud all over his face, an overjoyed **JET** looks up to see Scoot, Tucker, and the 🐸 looking at him. Once again, the 🐸 responds, "rib bit." "I think he is trying to tell us that his name is, 'Ribbit'," **JET** says confidently. Shaking her head, Scoot says with a smile, "looks like another muddy day at the park."

A day at the park always includes a visit to the [pond] to see their friends, the [ducks]. Out of nowhere, a green [frog] catches **JET's** attention with a deep, rumbling, "rib bit."

Swiftly, Scoot pulls a  from her  and catches the scoop of , gently placing it back on top of **JET's** . "That was nifty how you caught my , Scoot. "Ummmm, but..did I see you pull a  out of your ?" "Yupper doodles, you sure did," Scoot says sweetly.

"Huh!" says **JET**, rubbing his head.

All of a sudden,
Scoot sees that scoop of , hurling straight toward her!

top of the [swings],

JET is eating his
with a bit too much
silliness. 1-lick, 2-licks...
"Ooohhh nooo,"
JET cries out.

JET & **Scoot** enjoy their favorite things at the park:

, , and .

Balancing on

"Holy cow! How did you do that, Scoot?" Scoot replies, "It's nothing really; just a dash of daring and a smidge of spark." **"YOU ARE AWESOME!!!" JET** exclaims. With his engine running stronger than ever, **JET** through the clouds. Ringing his 🔔 he hollers, "Scoot you're the BOMB!" "It's no trouble at all," Scoot responds merrily. With Tucker warming up his legs and Scoot organizing herself, the threesome punch-it to the park.

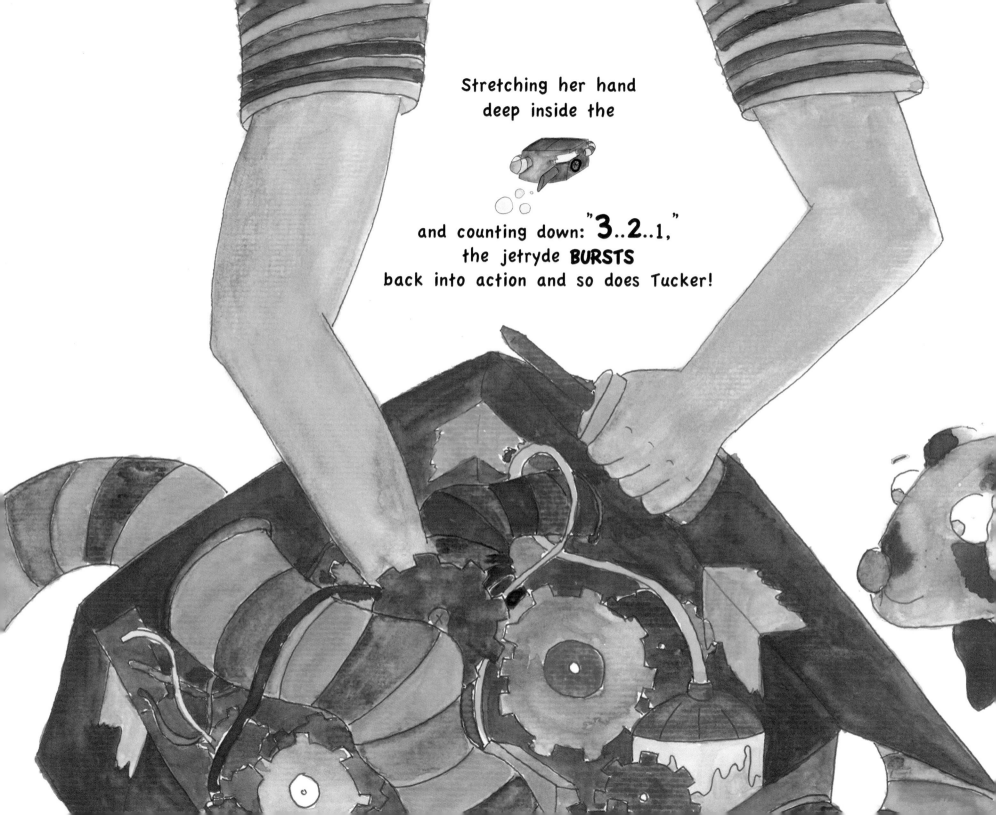

Stretching her hand
deep inside the

and counting down: "3..2..1,"
the jetryde **BURSTS**
back into action and so does Tucker!

As Scoot glides over the bridge and JET zooms through the ⬭, suddenly, sounds of engine trouble fill the sky. Scoot slooowly looks up to see...

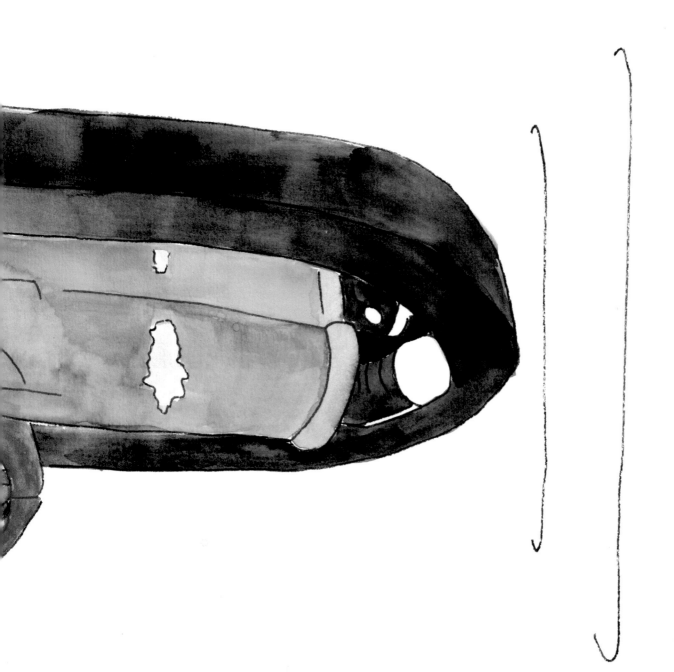

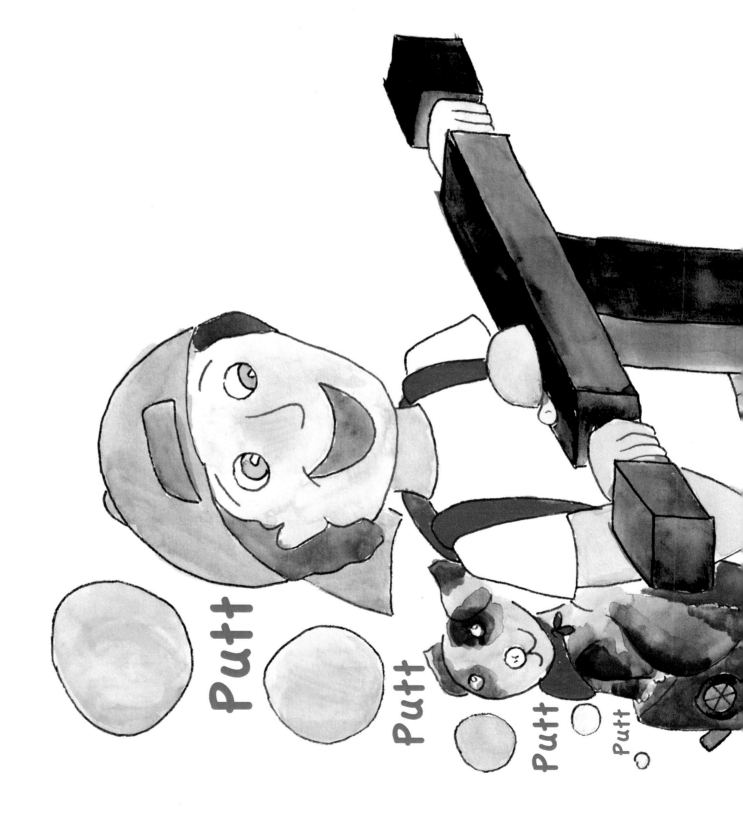

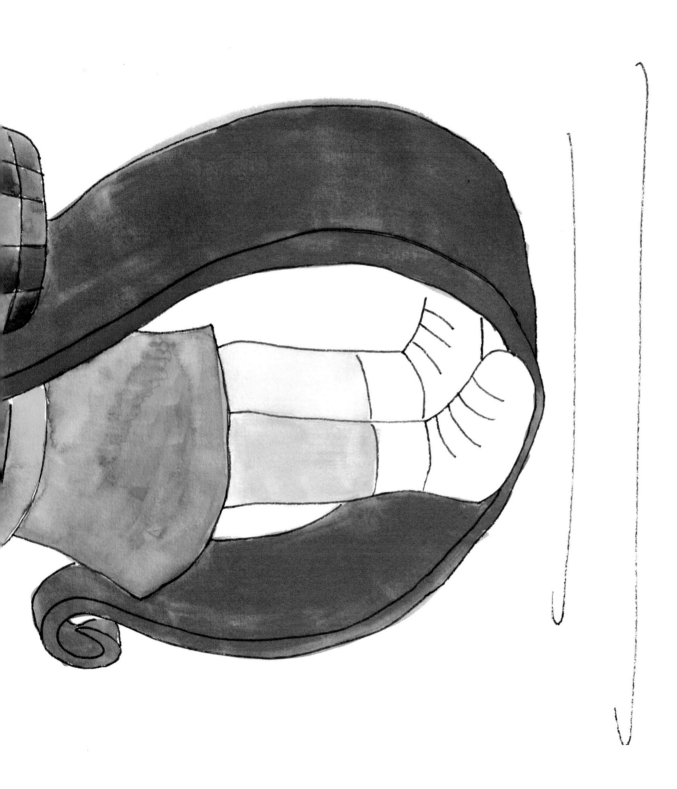

JET dresses as fast as he can... and .

Then sliding down on the handrail, **JET** pops off the banister and lands running straight for the kitchen **starving!!!**

For **Scoot**, getting ready in the morning is nice and organized. She likes to be ready in advance, so she lays out her outfit the night before:

and .

Scoot is giddy to spend Adventure-Saturday with **JET**, because it's always a fun day.

Skipping out of her room, she hops down each step counting out loud...

1 BOOM!

2 BOOM!

3

BOOM!

Arriving downstairs perfectly on for her

JET & Scoot meet at their special spot.
Scoot glides up on her POOSH bike, while
JET'S jetryde is pumping out perfectly clear
bubbles, idling just above the ground.

"Hi Scoot, what's buzzing?"
JET says excitedly, while giving
the 🔔 on his handlebar a good "Ring."

"Hi **JET!** Today is going to be
peeeaaachy," Scoot says cheerfully,
while patting Tucker's head.

"Want to go to the park?"
JET asks. "I sure do,"
Scoot replies. "Swell!" says **JET.**

"You fixed my jetryde and caught my ice cream, which saved Adventure-Saturday. Thank you," **JET** says kindly.

"You're welcome, I just wanted to keep our day rolling along. Besides, spending Adventure-Saturday together is what makes it so much fun," says **Scoot**.

If a sunset is the promise of a new beginning,
then this sunset is the promise of another new
Adventure-Saturday for JET & Scoot and Tucker.

Thanks for
coming along.
Until next
time...

PHRASE KEY

"Full bark talk" - Tucker's idea of a lively conversation with JET

"Holy cow" - an exclamation of surprise, shock

"Buzzing" - What's new?

"Cheese Whiz" - said to express frustration

"You're the BOMB" - really cool, you're so awesome, thanks for helping me

"Yupperdoodles" - An enthusiastic YES!

"Okey Dokey Artichokey" - a humorous way to agree with someone

"Just like downtown" - Means a place of excitement, where the lights
                        are bright and there is shopping and entertainment.